W9-BGT-981

The Circle

Bentley Little

Bentley Little

CEMETERY DANCE PUBLICATIONS

Baltimore
❖ 2012 ❖

FIRST EDITION
ISBN: 978-1-58767-300-9
Cemetery Dance Publications Edition 2012

The Circle
Copyright © 2002 Bentley Little
Dust jacket illustration by Steve Upham
Dust jacket design by Gail Cross
Typesetting and book design by Robert Morrish
All rights reserved. Manufactured in the United States of America

Cemetery Dance Publications
132-B Industry Lane, Unit 7
Forest Hill, MD 21050
Email: info@cemeterydance.com
www.cemeterydance.com

HELEN

It was hard to hear the knocking over the noise of the microwave, so Helen wasn't sure how long it had been going on, but the moment her oatmeal finished cooking she heard the staccato tapping of knuckles on wood, and she strode quickly out of the kitchen and through the living room to the front door. The knocking grew louder, harder, faster as she approached. Whoever was outside wanted desperately to get in, and while her first impulse was to throw open the door and let the knocker find refuge in her home, good sense won out, and she called, "Who is it?"

"Let me in!"

It was a child's voice, a boy's, and Helen found that she was not surprised. Something about the uninhibited ferocity of the knocking indicated a non-adult origin.

"Let me in!"

The kid sounded agitated, scared, and she imagined him being chased by bullies or pursued by an abusive father. Maybe he was fleeing a psychotic killer, like that kid who'd temporarily gotten away from Jeffrey Dahmer before the police had stupidly given him back to the cannibal. Helen unhooked the latch, threw the deadbolt and pulled open the door. She had time to register that he was small, nine maybe or ten, dirty, wearing nothing but a brown loincloth, and then he was speeding past her, running as fast as he could through her living room and down the hall.

"Hey!"

She tried to follow after him, but the bathroom door was already slammed shut and locked by the time she reached the hallway. There was something unnerving about that. The kid had not hesitated, had seemed to know exactly where he was going, as though he were intimately familiar with their house.

Helen knocked on the door. "Are you all right in there?"

No answer.

She knocked again. "Hello?"

The kid didn't answer, and she wondered if she should dial 911, call the police. What if there was something seriously wrong? She'd only gotten a glimpse of him when he dashed past her, and while he'd looked unhurt, maybe he was injured and she just hadn't seen it.

"Are you okay?"

There was no response, and she jiggled the knob. Worried that he had collapsed or passed out in there, she pressed her ear to the door. From inside, she heard grunting, straining, heard the disgusting sound of plopping water.

He was going to the bathroom.

Maybe he was sick, suffering from some intestinal disorder.

She moved away from the door, wondering if she should call Tony on his cell phone and have him come home. He'd only left ten minutes ago; he couldn't be at the office yet. Besides, maybe he'd have some ideas—

Suddenly the door burst open and the loinclothed kid was running past her down the hall.

She hadn't heard the door unlock, hadn't heard any noises at all, but she didn't have time to think about that and quickly followed him through the hallway, through the kitchen and out the back door. He sped across the yard and into the garage, slamming the small garage door behind him.

What the hell is going on here? Helen stood on the stoop, torn between going back and checking the bathroom to make sure nothing was amiss, and following the boy into the garage to make sure he was all right. She finally moved forward and hurried across the lawn. To her surprise, the door was locked. She wasn't aware that it *could* be locked; the door was old and practically falling off its hinges, the pressboard peeling away in buckling layers beneath the flaking paint. She tried turning the knob but it was frozen, tried pulling on the door but it was shut tight. She could go inside and get the key for the Master Lock on the big garage door, but by that time he could be gone.

Theirs was an old garage, with a small window on the side, and she walked around the corner of the building and peered through the glass, trying to make out what was what behind the decades-thick layer of dirt. She saw the boy, in the open area between Tony's tools and lawnmower and the piled bulk of summer lawn furniture.

He was squatting on the floor, grimacing, obviously trying to go again.

Helen thought for a brief second, then glanced around the backyard until she found what she was looking for: the used cinderblocks that Tony had scavenged last week. They were piled against the fence and already covered with dead leaves and spiderwebs, but she grabbed the top one and placed it against the small door, pushing it hard against the wood. The door opened outward, and if she could put enough weight against it, the boy would not be able to get out.

Six trips back and forth, and she had all the cinderblocks piled in front of the door. She took one last look through the window—he was still squatting, still straining—then ran back into the house. She went directly to the bathroom and looked into the toilet, grimacing, prepared for the worst. She saw—

—diamonds.

Helen blinked dumbly. There were not just a few stones; there was a pile of them, a small mound at the bottom of the still clear water, their facets shimmering in the room's yellowish light. There was only one explanation for their origin, one place from which they could have come, and though she tried to think of an alternate answer, there did not seem to be one.

The boy shit diamonds.

It was the only possibility.

She reached into the water, picked up one that was as big as the fingernail on her thumb. She wasn't a lapidary expert or a gemologist; she probably couldn't tell a real diamond from a cubic zirconium. But she placed the stone against the bathroom mirror and drew it down. A long scratch followed in its wake. Diamonds cut glass. That's all the proof she needed.

Helen was already late for work, but she grabbed the cordless phone in the kitchen and rather than calling her office dialed her husband as she hurried out the back door. He answered on the second ring, and she quickly told him what had happened, how the dirty loinclothed boy had been pounding on the front door and she'd let him inside and he'd run straight to the bathroom and locked himself in.

"I heard him…*going,*" she said. "I thought he was sick or something, like he had intestinal problems. Then he ran out the back door and into the garage." She paused. "The kid poops diamonds."

"Hold on, hold on, hold on." She could imagine him shaking his head with his eyes half-closed in that annoying way he had. "What did you say?"

"The kid poops diamonds." She knew how it sounded. Hell, it didn't make much sense even to her. But there it was. It happened, it *was* happening, and no amount of analyzing or rationalization could change the cold hard fact that there was a pile of diamonds sitting in the bottom of their toilet bowl.

Helen took a deep breath. "When the boy goes to the bathroom, diamonds come out. Big, perfectly cut diamonds. They're in the toilet of the small bathroom right now. And he's in the garage. That's why I called you. What do you think I should do?"

"I have that meeting with Fincher today, Hel." His voice had suddenly dropped to a low whisper, and she knew his boss was now in the room. "Do I have to come home? Do I have to come right now?"

"Tony!"

"Call Child Services or something. Look it up in the phone book. Let them take care of him. Go across the street and wake up Gil Marotta if you're scared. He's home all day. He can help you."

"I'm not scared! I told you, he craps diamonds. The kid sat on our toilet, and went to the bathroom and diamonds literally came out of his ass."

"Hel…"

"I'm serious." She lowered her voice, though there was no one to overhear. "We're rich, Tony. I have him trapped in the garage right now—"

"Trapped!"

"Just 'til we figure out what to do."

"That's kidnapping!"

She was in front of the garage, and she pressed her foot against the stacked cinderblocks, gratified to find that they did not budge. "He went in there himself and he hasn't even tried to get out."

"But if he did try to get out, he couldn't. You've trapped him."

"That's why I called you."

There was a frustrated exhalation that sounded like static. "Call someone. The city, the county, the state. One of them has a department to deal with runaways and missing children. Hand him over to them. Your diamonds…" He exhaled again, and she knew he didn't believe her. "Do what you want with the diamonds. I'll look at them when I get home."

"Okay. Bye." She clocked off without waiting for a reply and stared for a moment at the peeling door. If he didn't believe her, what *did* he think? The only other alternative was that she was lying. Or crazy.

She didn't even want to consider that. Her world had been turned upside down as it was; the last thing she needed was to find out that Tony, to whom she'd entrusted her deepest, most secret feelings over the past fifteen years, to whom she'd made passionate love this morning before getting out of bed, could so quickly and easily be persuaded that she had lost her mind.

She walked around the side of the garage and tried to focus instead on the diamonds. They were worth a fortune. Thousands of dollars. Hundreds of thousands. Millions, maybe. But how would they explain the fact that they were in possession of the rocks? did they have to explain it? She didn't know. Her knowledge of this stuff came entirely from movies and television, and while the jewelers to whom they sold the diamonds might not ask any questions, the IRS most certainly would. They'd have to be able to explain where they got this sudden wealth, this huge increase of income.

It was all confusing, and she peered through the dirty window into the garage.

The boy was squatting on the floor and shitting again.

Rubies.

Even in the dim refracted light they glittered redly, and Helen wondered how such a thing was physically possible. It wasn't, she knew, and she watched as rubies dropped onto the cement floor. One, two, three...

Maybe they had a miracle on their hands. She and Tony weren't religious, and she'd never been one to believe in any sort of supernatural claptrap, but there was nothing in the known world that could explain what was happening here, and she found herself thinking that maybe they were being rewarded, maybe this was a gift that had been sent to them from some higher power.

Inside the garage, the boy grimaced, and another ruby was squeezed out from between the cheeks of his buttocks.

Tony called after his meeting, just before noon, and Helen lied and said that she'd phoned Social Services, the Child Protection division, and a caseworker was here with her now. In truth, she was still perched outside the garage, making sure the boy did not escape. He was asleep, curled into a fetal position in the center of the open space to the right of Tony's record boxes, but he had already produced emeralds and some gemstone she didn't recognize in addition to the diamonds and rubies.

She'd brought out a folding chair and today's newspaper, as well as a water bottle and a bag of potato chips. No telling how long she was going to be out here, and she figured she might as well make herself comfortable.

She'd had plenty of time to think this morning, and she'd revised her theory as to the boy's origin. He was not a divine miracle sent to reward them for some good deed or morally upright behavior. He was a natural phenomenon who had fallen into their grasp, and if they were smart enough and savvy enough, he would make them rich.

But where had he been before this? she couldn't help but wonder. And who had had him before? Weren't those people looking for him, trying to get him back? In her mind, she saw a bunch of bumbling business-suited crooks led by Joe Flynn or Cesar Romero, like in all those old Disney movies.

Tony took off work early, and she was inside the house for a quick bathroom break when he arrived home just after three. She was using the bathroom in the master bedroom, having left the diamonds in the toilet untouched in the bathroom off the hall, and when she heard him call tentatively, "Helen?" she quickly finished and met him in the living room.

"Everything all squared away?" he asked when he saw her. "That kid gone?"

"Actually," she told him, "he's in the garage."

"What?"

"Now we have emeralds and rubies and, I think, sapphires and topaz. At least, that's what the pictures in the encyclopedia look like, but it's hard to tell."

"You didn't call anyone? You kept him prisoner in the fucking *garage?*"

Helen had never heard him so angry, and for a second she thought he might actually hit her. But instead he smacked his own forehead, palm hitting head skin with an audible slap, then ran his fingers so hard through his hair that it pulled up his eyebrows. "What the hell has gotten into you?"

"Come here." She led him down the hall to the bathroom and showed him the diamonds in the toilet. He reached in wonderingly and picked up a small handful, holding them up to the light.

"Jesus."

"I told you." She smiled and could not keep the excitement out of her voice. "We're rich."

Tony shook his head, carefully putting the diamonds down on the counter next to the hairspray. "That's still no reason to lock up that poor boy in the garage. He's not a rabid animal."

"No, but he's wild. He's—"

"I'm getting him out." Tony pulled off his tie as he walked, throwing it on the table in the breakfast nook as he headed through the kitchen and out the door. Helen followed, feeling chastened and embarrassed and…something else. Afraid? Maybe so, though she didn't know why. She stood on the lawn, not helping but not hindering, as he removed the stacked cinderblocks from in front of the door.

"Hello?" Tony announced. "Are you okay in there?" But there was no answer.

He carefully opened the garage door—

And the boy ran out.

"Catch him!" Helen yelled instinctively, and for a brief confused moment Tony tried to do just that, but the dirty loinclothed child slipped between his hands, ran around the lemon tree and darted into the oleander bushes that hid the chain-link fence separating their yard from the woman's house next door.

Tony moved up to the bushes, carefully parting branches, looking for the boy but apparently not finding him. He moved all the way to the back fence and the end of the oleanders, but the boy seemed to have disappeared.

"You think he went next door?" Helen asked.

"I don't see how. The branches are all tangled in the fence; I don't see how he could get over it. Maybe there's a hole underneath the fence that I missed..."

"What do we do now? Do you still think we should call someone?"

Tony thought for a moment, shook his head. She could see that the decision weighed on him, that he felt uneasy about it. "Since you imprisoned him all day long in our garage, I'm not that anxious to announce our connection to him," he said. "Let someone else take care of it. Let the next person figure out what to do with him. It's out of our hands now."

Helen smiled. "And we're rich."

She walked into the garage to gather up the rubies and the emeralds and all the other gems.

* * *

They still hadn't told anyone else about their newfound riches. They hadn't even bothered to find out the going rate for precious stones. They had weighed their haul, however, placing each type of gemstone in a separate sack and placing the sacks on the bathroom scale to get a rough approximation of what they had.

Helen had decided to quit her job and never go back to work. She had not called in sick today, and no one from the office had called home to inquire about her, so she figured she just wouldn't show up again. They could send her last check through the mail.

Tony was not so optimistic. These could be fake jewels, he told her. They could be stolen.

He was planning to go to work tomorrow as always.

It was late. They'd stayed up far longer than intended, talking about what had happened, debating what to do, but not really coming to any conclusions. Too tired for her usual shower, Helen took off her clothes and put on her nightshirt. "Where do you think he went?" she wondered. She pressed her face to the bedroom window, placing her hands on both sides of her face to filter out the glare and reflection from the inside lights. It was completely dark at first, black, but then her eyes adjusted and she could make out the lemon tree, the storage shed, the oleanders.

The boy.

He was crouched in the bushes, staring at the house, staring at *her*, and his eyes seemed to be luminescent.

She nearly jumped, her heart leaping in her chest. A chill passed through her, and though she didn't know why she was scared, she was, and she wished to God that she had not decided to peek out the window.

His eyes were still staring, unblinking, and she thought that he was probably taking a shit.

What had seemed magical and wondrous in the daytime now seemed spooky and vaguely sinister. Why had he come back? Why hadn't he left for good? What did he want?

"What is it?" Tony asked from the bed.

She was afraid to move away from the glass, afraid to let him out of her sight. "He's out there. The boy. He's in the oleanders, staring at me. I can see him."

Tony scrambled out of bed, rushed over, but in the few seconds it took him to reach her, the boy looked to the right, his luminescent eyes shifting in a different direction…and then he was gone. She squinted at the spot where he had been, looked to the left, to the right, but he was nowhere to be seen. It was dark outside and he could have easily slid into the shadows, could be hiding right in plain sight, but somehow she didn't think that that was the case.

There was the sound of frantic knocking on the front door.

"Don't let him in!" she screamed at Tony. She pushed him away from her, pushed him toward the bedroom door, and he started running, spurred by the urgency in her voice. "Make sure everything's locked! Make sure he can't get inside!"

She didn't know what had gotten into her, why she was suddenly so frightened by the child, but she had always been one to trust her instincts, and she wasn't about to question her reactions now. She had pulled back from the window, and the outside world was just a uniform black with her own reflection, horrified and ghostlike, on the glass.

The knocking on the front door had stopped, and she held her breath, listening, heart racing. She wanted to yell at Tony not to open the door under any circumstances, not even to open it a crack to see what was going on outside, but she was afraid to call out in case he had already done so.

What if the boy was in the house?

So what if he was? He'd been in here this morning and the only thing he'd done was leave them with enough diamonds to ensure that they would never have to work again.

Of course, that was before she'd trapped him in the hot garage all day long without food or water.

"Let me in."

She started at the sound of the voice. It was clear and close, and when she looked at the window, she saw the boy's dirty face next to the glass. She backed carefully toward the bed, afraid to look away.

"Let me in," the boy said, and this time his voice was a sly whisper that should not have been able to penetrate the closed window.

"No!" she screamed.

"Let me in."

They were the only words he said, the only words she'd ever heard him say, and she wondered now if that meant something, if he was like a vampire or a witch or whatever that monster was that had to be invited inside before it could do any harm. God, she hoped so.

The backyard light was flipped on, illuminating the lawn area and the patio and the front of the garage. Tony. He was in the kitchen. "Don't go outside!" she yelled. "Stay in! Don't go out!" He didn't respond, but the back door didn't open, so she assumed that he'd heard her.

In the glare of the floodlight, she could see the boy more clearly. He had moved away from the window and was squatting on the grass, going again. He cried out in pain—he was obviously passing something large—and while Helen watched, something big and dark dropped from between his legs. vaguely round, it rolled a few inches, then stopped, caught on a straight irregular side. He reached underneath him and lifted it up.

By its hair.

Helen's hand automatically went to her mouth, and she backed away from the window, her legs threatening to buckle beneath her. The boy had just shit a human head.

She still hadn't gotten a good look at it, but it was female, she could tell that much, and—

Oh, God, he was bringing it up to the window to show her!

Let me in, the child's lips were saying, but either no sound was coming out or she couldn't hear the words. He was holding the head high, like a lantern, and when he reached a spot where the floodlight's beam was not obstructed by the roof of the house, she saw that it had her own face; eyes wide, mouth open in an expression of surprise that no doubt echoed her own.

The boy threw the head at the window, and with a frightened yelp Helen ran across the bedroom to the door. Behind her, she heard it hit the glass: a muffled thump followed by a sickening squeegee sound. Was it sliding down the window? She had to turn and look, but all she saw was the boy picking up the head—

her head

—by its hair and cocking his arm to throw it again.

Let me in, his lips mouthed.

She ran into the dark hallway but stopped almost immediately. Where was Tony? He should have been back. He should have returned by now. But the house was silent. She didn't hear his voice, didn't hear his footfalls on the creaking floor.

Maybe he'd been captured. Or killed. Maybe there was an army of these boys, all look-alikes, and when the first one had run off, he'd gone to get his friends and now they were back and out for revenge.

Behind her, in the bedroom, the head—

her head

—hit the glass again.

Helen screamed, a wrenching gut-deep cry of terror and frustration, and Tony came running out of the kitchen, into the hall. She threw herself at him, held on tight. "Thank God," she sobbed. "Thank God."

"I was watching him through the kitchen window," Tony said, and he sounded rattled, his voice shaky. "He was...he..."

"He shit a head!" Helen cried. "*My* head! And now he's throwing it at our bedroom window trying to get in!" She looked up into her husband's face. "Why's he doing this? What the hell is he?"

"I don't know," Tony admitted.

Behind them, in the bedroom, the head hit the glass.

"Don't let him in!" Helen said, clutching Tony tightly. "Whatever you do, don't let him in!"

"I won't."

"Let's call the police," she suggested. "I'll tell them everything. I'll show them the diamonds and the rubies and…and… everything."

She blinked, stopped.

The diamonds. The rubies. The emeralds. The sapphires. The topaz. They were still in the house, wrapped up in bags in the den. But were they still the same? The boy had changed with the coming of night, turned into something else. Had the gemstones changed, too? Were they now eyes and teeth and fingers? Somehow, such a thing wasn't hard to imagine.

Wiping her eyes, taking a deep shuddering breath, she pulled herself away from Tony and grabbed his hand, leading him into the den. She was prepared for anything, but the diamonds were still diamonds, the rubies still rubies, all was as it should have been.

The pounding had stopped. Either he'd broken through the window with the excreted head or he'd given up the tactic and was now trying to get in some other way. She knew that he would never give up completely. He might cease a specific action, but his ultimate goal would always remain the same.

Whatever that might be.

Tony was picking up the phone to dial 911 when suddenly there was noise all around them, a papery, whispery chittering that seemed to come from every side. He dropped the phone and they quickly ran out of the room, but the noise was in the hallway, too. And the living room.

"Come on!" he said, and led the way into the kitchen. Here, through the windows, they could see the bugs. There were hundreds of them, thousands, and they swarmed over the grass, over the patio, over the house, moving up the walls, starting to cover the windows. Even through the roof and ceiling she and Tony could hear the chittering sound, and Helen was about to ask why they were making such a weird noise when she finally figured it out.

They were trying to get inside by eating their way through.

"Oh, shit." Tony pointed outside. The boy was squatting and straining, and what dropped from between the cheeks of his buttocks this time was a cascade of pitch black beetles with visibly snapping pincers. They spread out, moving impossibly fast, and they kept coming, spewing out in a torrent. These were what was engulfing the house, and even as they watched, their view of the boy was obstructed as a black mass of moving beetles inched up the window glass.

Helen started crying again. Why had she opened the front door this morning? Why had she let that boy inside? If she had ignored him, he would have gone elsewhere and right now instead of fighting for their lives they would be peacefully sleeping in their bed, just like their neighbors were.

Their neighbors! If these beetles were covering the *whole* house, the other people on the circle should be able to see what was going on. Maybe one of them would come over and try to help, maybe one of them would call the police.

Of course, it *was* late. And the chance that anyone was up right now and looking out their front windows at their neighbors' houses was pretty damn slim.

Gil, maybe. He worked at night. He could come home and see what was happening and get help.

Tony, standing as far as possible from the blackening windows, was dialing 911 from the kitchen phone, but she could tell by the confused frown on his face that he was having no luck. The beetles had probably overrun the phone line and gnawed through it. He threw down the receiver, swearing.

"Where's the cell phone?" she cried.

"I left it in the car."

"Oh shit. Oh shit." Helen took a deep breath, swallowed her sobs. "What are we going to do?"

"I don't know." Tony got two big knives out of the top drawer, handed one to Helen. "Let's go to the front door. If it looks like we can make it, we run. If not, I guess we'll hole up in the small bathroom. It doesn't have any windows. It's probably the safest room in the house."

A loud screech cut through the low noise of the beetles. Or, rather, a loud series of concurrent screeches. The windows shattered, hundreds of the black bugs tumbling over the sink, over the counter onto the floor. Helen had time to register that the glass had broken in clean even lines; then the beetles were teeming over the breakfast nook, up the walls, onto the ceiling, a dark unstoppable wave.

She clutched Tony hard with her left hand while holding tight to the knife with her right, ready to slash at anything that came at her.

She was concentrating so hard on the hordes of beetles swarming over the floor that she neglected to keep track of the insects on the ceiling. When Tony's grip tightened on her own, however, and his knife motioned upward, she saw that the bugs had covered the area directly above them and were moving toward the open doorway into the hall. One fell on her knife hand, pincers clacking crazily. But it was the opposite end of the bug that rent her flesh, that sliced through the skin next to her thumb, and she saw, protruding from the beetle's hind end, a small sparkling diamond.

That was what had cut through the window glass, she realized.

More bugs started to fall, landing on her arms, her shoulders, her head. She tried to shake them off, tried to pull off the one in her palm, but the diamond was sunk into her flesh. Suddenly...it was released. The tiny gem was pushed into her and others followed, a steady stream of them.

The beetle was shitting diamonds inside her.

Screaming, jerking her shoulders, waving her knife wildly, Helen tried desperately to rid herself of the insects. Next to her, Tony was doing the same thing as beetles landed on his shoulders, scurrying both down his arms, and up his head. Pinpricks of pain erupted all over her skin as diamonds cut her, sinking into her skin, piercing through her clothes. She scraped some off of her left arm with the knife, but the diamonds remained embedded and more beetles took the place of the old ones.

She was going down.

And then the boy walked in. The insects had eaten through the door and part of the wall, and he stepped through the ragged hole, loincloth flapping, even his dirty skin looking bright against the blackness of the bugs. He carried nothing with him—no head, thank God—and the expression on his face was one of total and utter calm, a far cry from the wild agitation of the morning. His eyes still seemed luminescent, eerily so, and there was something in his poised slow approach that seemed defiantly unnatural. The wave of beetles parted before him, allowing him to pass, and even on the ceiling above a clear swath appeared.

Helen was sobbing, crying not so much from the pain but from the complete sense of defeat that had engulfed her and seemed to be the only emotion she could conjure. She closed her eyes...

And the bugs were gone.

She felt their absence instantly. There was no retreat, no movement, only what seemed to be a spontaneous disappearance. She opened her eyes—they could only have been closed for a few seconds—and the kitchen was clear. Evidence of their invasion still remained. The wall and door they had eaten. The scratches and welts all over her and Tony. They were not part of a false vision or hallucination. They'd been here. But she had no idea what had happened to them.

Tony was standing next to her, dead on his feet, still clutching the useless kitchen knife. Before them stood the boy, and he stared for a moment as if studying them.

"What do you want?" Helen cried.

The child smiled, and it was the most horrifying thing she had ever seen. Slowly, he squatted down on his haunches, shifting aside his loincloth, preparing to evacuate.

"NO!" Tony cried, his voice filled with terror.

Neither of them had any idea what was coming next, but they both knew that this was the end, the grand finale, the climax of what had begun this morning when Helen had allowed the desperate child into their home.

The boy grimaced, his face turning red, the muscles in his neck bulging, and what emerged from between his legs was—

a single red rose.

It arrived perfectly, petals intact, leaves on stem, though how that was possible Helen did not know. The flower was dark burgundy, with a single white spot on the topmost petal, and she recognized it immediately. A rose with exactly that rare coloration had been growing wild in the woman's yard next door. Helen had seen it last spring when they'd trimmed the oleanders. She'd reached over the chain-link fence with her clippers and cut the rose, thinking it would make a nice centerpiece for the dinner they were having that night with Fincher and his wife, but when she put it in a vase she saw that it was overrun with scores of nearly microscopic bugs, and she threw it outside in the garbage.

The two couldn't be connected...yet she knew that somehow they were. The boy took the flower in his fingers and with a flourish that seemed inappropriate for both his age and the circumstances, handed it to her.

Maybe this was it, she thought, maybe it would all be over now. She glanced at Tony, who nodded slightly. Sniffling, trying hard to rein in her emotions, she reached out and accepted the proffered rose. A thorn stabbed her thumb, and where her blood touched the plant, it withered, blackened. She looked into the center of the flower and saw that it was crawling with teeny tiny bugs, and when she squinted and looked closer at them, she saw that they were miniature versions of the beetles that had been attacking her and Tony.

The boy started dancing. "Let me in!" he said/sang, and rather than a request or a demand, it was a jubilant announcement, a celebratory taunt. *They* let me in, he was proclaiming, although he left off that first word. "Let me in!" he said/sang/danced.

Suddenly, the child stopped dancing and doubled over in pain. A harsh spasm wracked his body and he fell to the floor. It looked like he was being hit with a hammer, and though she knew that was impossible, so many other impossible things had happened that she thought it might be true.

Yes! she thought.

She hoped that invisible hammer beat the hell out of him.

With each blow or spasm, the boy seemed to diminish slightly. He wasn't growing smaller or shrinking; he was becoming less human, his legs looking more spindly, his arms shortening and losing inner solidity, the features of his face fading into blandness. He rolled toward the hole in the wall and door through which he'd come, still buffeted by the physical impact of something unseen, and by the time he reached the ragged opening, she could not see any mouth or nose or eyes. He looked like a large piece of Silly Putty shaped into the general form of a person and tied with a piece of dirty cloth.

Then he was outside and gone, and with grateful relief, Helen threw aside the rose and collapsed into the arms of her husband. Tony was battered and bleeding, but his arms were strong and felt good, and both of them looked toward the hole in the wall, waiting to see what, if anything, would come through it next.

When several minutes passed with no sign of movement, no sound from outside, Tony, holding her tightly, limped toward the ragged opening and looked into the backyard. It was clear. No boy, no head, no bugs, nothing.

It was over.

They didn't know what had happened, didn't know how or why it had stopped, but they were grateful that it had and, still leaning on each other, they made their way through the house to make sure they saw nothing out of the ordinary. They didn't. In the den, the bags of gemstones lay on top of Tony's desk, undisturbed. They had not disappeared, not turned to shit, they were what they had always been: diamonds, rubies, emeralds, sapphire, topaz.

Helen refused to touch them. She turned back around, returned to the hallway. "Give them away," she said. "Throw them away."

She never wanted to see another jewel or gemstone again.

Tony nodded tiredly.

Neither of them seemed to know what to do next. It was late, they were exhausted, and they should probably clean up, tend to their wounds and go back to bed, but instead they stood there for several moments, leaning against the wall in the hallway. After awhile, Helen started to notice a distinct pressure in her abdomen, an uncomfortable yet very familiar urge. She looked at the clotting wounds on her arms, saw the sparkle of diamonds in the drying blood. Next to her, Tony shifted uneasily, pressing his legs together, bending forward slightly. She looked at him.

"I have to go to the bathroom," Tony admitted. "And I'm afraid to."

"Me, too." Helen felt a sharp cramping in her bowels, and wondered what was in there, what would come out.

"We have to go sometime."

Across from them was the bathroom. The light in there was on, but that did not lessen the ominous atmosphere. She thought that she would never forget the sight of those diamonds in the clear water, piled like a pyramid.

"I'll go first," Helen said. She walked over to the bathroom, stepped inside. Looking at the toilet, she felt a sharp cramp, then turned back toward Tony. "Wish me luck," she told him.

"Luck," he said softly.
She closed the door behind her.

FRANK

"It tastes like honey."

"Nuh-uh."

"It says so right here. 'His tongue slid into her moist opening, and he tasted her delicious golden nectar, the sweet honey of her love.'"

Chase shook his head. "My brother's *done* it. And he says it tastes like sweat."

Johnny and Frank looked at each other. "Ewwww," they said simultaneously.

"You guys're like a fucking cartoon show." Chase grabbed the book from Frank's hands and tossed it back into the closet with the others, covering up the pile with a load of dirty clothes.

Frank picked up his Coke from the floor and finished it off, tossing the can at the wastepaper basket and missing. That's what he liked about hanging out at Chase's house—the boy's parents were never home.

They always had the place to themselves. They could do cool stuff like read porno books or go to chat rooms on the Internet or make prank phone calls. That wasn't possible at his and Johnny's houses. Johnny's mom didn't work, so she was always home. His own mom did work and was gone, but since his dad worked at night, he was home all day. That was the worst.

But Chase's house was open range, they were free to do whatever they wanted, and it was almost like they weren't kids, like they were college students rooming together, grown-up buddies hanging out in their own pad.

"Why should we believe your brother?" Johnny said. "Maybe he's lying and the book's telling the truth."

"Because I know him. Because I caught him in his room with a babe once when my parents were gone. And because he doesn't just *talk* about things like you two dweebs. He actually does 'em."

"Us two dweebs?" Frank said, smiling.

"Yeah," Johnny said. "Between school and sleeping and hanging around with us, I don't see where you have a whole hell of a lot of extra time."

"All right, like *us,*" Chase said, giving in. He finished his own Coke, threw the can in the air and karate kicked it across the room, where it hit the edge of a table and landed on the carpet. He looked from Frank to Johnny. "You know, we have a chance to change all that."

"All what?"

"I overheard my brother talking on the phone. He and his friend Paul are going to the shrine tonight. They're going to try to use it."

The shrine.

Frank glanced at Johnny, then looked quickly away. Neither of them had ever seen the shrine, but they'd known about it ever since they were in grammar school. It was in the backyard of that lady professor's house, next to Johnny's, and rumor had it that she was a witch. Such rumors were understandable. Her house looked like it ought to be condemned, which was weird for someone with a job like hers, and she was hugely fat. Hardly anyone ever saw her, and when they did, it was only very briefly as she got in or out of her car. She taught about ancient religions or something at the junior college, and supposedly she'd put up the shrine to worship her gods. According to Keri Armstrong, who'd moved in fifth grade but who used to live on the opposite side of the witch's house and was the only one of them brave enough to go into that overgrown backyard on a truth-or-dare, the shrine could grant wishes. If you wished the right way and said the right words and did the right things, it would give you what you wanted. A lot of kids had talked about using it over the years, but as far as he knew, none of them had ever been brave enough to go through with it.

"What are they going to do?" Johnny asked.

"They want money. Chaz has his eye on this old Charger that he said him and Paul can rebuild. They found it in *The Recycler*, even went down to look at it, but it's two grand and in shit shape, and they'll need another grand just to get it to work. So they're going to ask for three thousand."

Frank whistled.

"Yeah, I know."

"It's not gonna work."

"No." Chase flopped down on the couch. "You think that cow's really a witch?"

"There's no such thing as witches."

"I know that, dill weed. I mean, do you think *she* thinks she's a witch? Obviously she doesn't have magic powers or anything. Otherwise, she wouldn't be so fat and her house wouldn't be such a goddamn mess. But if she thinks she does, she might still do all those spells and potions and things, even if they don't work, just because it's part of her religion or whatever." He leaned forward conspiratorially. "Maybe she sacrifices cats or dogs on that altar."

"Or kids," Johnny said, putting into words what they'd been thinking.

"Or kids," Chase agreed solemnly.

They considered that for a moment.

"So what's your plan?" Johnny asked excitedly.

They both knew Chase had a plan. He never suggested they do anything without having some detailed scheme in mind, and they knew he didn't want to just spy on his brother and his brother's friends. Frank feigned an enthusiasm he did not feel. "Yeah. What's the plan?"

Chase grinned. "We follow 'em out there, see what happens, see if they get their money. If they do, we ask for a hot chick for ourselves."

"You just said it wasn't going to work."

"It probably won't. And if it doesn't, we'll throw some rocks at 'em and scare 'em. They'll be just as freaked by that place as us and they'll probably crap their pants. If it *does* work..." He raised his eyebrows comically.

"But..." Johnny said. He thought for a moment. "The shrine. How does it...operate? Do you just pray to it or do you have to bring it something or what?"

"I'm not sure," Chase admitted.

Frank didn't like anything about this. He didn't believe in magical powers or the supernatural, but...still. "What if it's a Monkey's Paw-type deal? What if it gives you what you want but in some way that punishes you? Like your brother gets his money but it's because your parents die in a car crash and he inherits the cash? Or you ask for a babe and she's a corpse or something?"

"*I* ask for a babe? *We* ask for a babe."

"Whatever."

It was obvious that Chase had not thought through any of these possibilities, and though Frank hoped that he'd been able to scare his friend, that Chase might change his mind and cancel the whole thing, it was obvious from the expression on his face that the other boy gave such concerns only the briefest of considerations before deciding to go through with his original plan.

Since Chase didn't know exactly when his brother would be heading over to the shrine, only knew that it would be late and long after dark, he suggested they all meet in his side yard at nine sharp, next to the fence where they used to have their clubhouse.

Frank shuffled his feet and looked down at the ground, refusing to meet Chase's eyes. "I might not be able to make it," he said. "If I'm not there by nine, you guys go on without me."

"Whaddaya mean, you might not make it? It's Friday night, dude! What are you going to do, stay inside and watch TV with your mommy?"

The truth was, that sounded a whole hell of a lot better than sneaking through the witch's backyard to spy on Chase's brother. But he didn't want to be tagged for life as a pussy and a momma's boy.

"Listen," Johnny said, "we'll tell our parents we're going to a movie." He looked at Frank. "I'll say that your mom's driving us; you tell your parents that my mom's taking us." It was tacitly acknowledged that Chase would have no problem getting out of his house.

Frank snorted. "You don't think my parents'll look out the window and notice that your parents' car's still in the driveway? You're two houses away! Jesus, what a stupid plan."

"Sneak out," Chase said. "I don't care how you do it; the details are up to you. Just make sure that you're there on time." He looked from Johnny to Frank. "You understand?"

Both boys nodded.

"Good. Because, trust me, there'll be hell to pay if you don't show."

* * *

They met at the appointed time in Chase's side yard, where Chase was keeping an eye on his brother's bedroom window. Chaz and Paul were still in there, and Chase said he thought they were waiting for another friend, but almost immediately after he said that, the bedroom light went out and a moment later the two older boys walked out the front door.

"The front door? I had to sneak out my window!" Johnny complained.

Frank had, too, although escape from the house had been much easier than he thought. It was the first time he'd ever done such a thing, and the only thing he was worried about was getting the screen back on the window when he returned.

"Come on!" Chase whispered. "Let's go!"

They followed Chaz and Paul as the older boys walked down the sidewalk, around the circle, the three of them keeping to the shadows, staying on lawns, darting from bush to bush. Chaz and Paul were acting casual, but they were acting *too* casual, and it was clear that they'd planned this thing out in advance. When they reached the witch's house, they walked past it, stopped, pretended to talk, then walked back in front of it again. They were obviously on the lookout, making sure they had not been spotted, and when they determined that the coast was clear, they ran into the overgrown front yard.

The darkness seemed to swallow them. Frank knew it was only the power of suggestion, a holdover from his younger days, when he'd been afraid to even look at that house and yard at night, but it seemed to him that illumination from the streetlight in front of Johnny's died right at the edge of the witch's property line, that light was not allowed on that wild weedy stretch of ground.

"Hurry up!" Chase had brought a flashlight but he didn't want to use it, not unless he had to. He thought it would give them away, and he sped after his brother and Paul, darting from dead tree to dead bush, pushing through the high dry weeds toward the side of the house. When they were far enough back from the road and thought no one would be able to see, Chaz and Paul switched on their own flashlights, and from that point on it was easier to trail them.

They moved past a broken lawnmower and a discarded washing machine, a tree stump and a pile of buckets, and then they were in the backyard. There was no wall, no gate, no barrier of any kind, and it was only by the position of the fence next door that they knew where they were. They passed behind the edge of the house, and back here, if possible, the yard was even more of a mess. Frank understood now why neighbors had gotten up petitions against the woman, trying to make her clean up her place. It *smelled,* for Christ's sake. Like her sewer had backed up or like she and all of the neighborhood cats and dogs had just taken a dump back here. Next to him he heard Johnny, the most squeamish member of their trio, gagging as though he were about to puke.

"Shhh!" Chase warned.

The debris and the foliage both grew thicker as they tried to follow the intermittent glow of the flashlight. This was a big yard, Frank thought, much bigger than any of theirs, and already he was lost, his sense of direction all screwed up. High bushes, and piles of wood and old rotting newspapers blocked the view of any of the adjoining yards, and even the black bulk of the house was lost from sight. They passed by a mountain of dead leaves, a bunch of scrap metal and chicken wire, and a pile of cardboard boxes filled with garbage. They seemed to be going in circles, and it occurred to him that Chaz and his friend didn't know where the shrine was either; they were just searching by trial-and-error.

Then they were there.

Chase, in the front, stopped and crouched down behind an upside-down birdbath. Frank and Johnny followed suit. Chaz trained his flashlight on the shrine. Frank wasn't sure what he thought it would look like, but it had been more like those things in the Chinese restaurant or in his friend Thanh's house: a red alcove with a little plastic statue inside it and some gaudy Asian doodads hanging from the top, little post sitting in the front with some burning sticks of incense.

This, though, was…different.

For one thing, it was big, as tall as he was, rather than a little box that came up to his knee. And it looked old. It was sort of an arch shape or a tombstone shape, and it was made out of mud or adobe or cheap cement that was all flaking off and crumbling. At the top was some sort of design, a squiggly spiral that was carved into the deteriorating material. Below that was a rounded alcove that was either painted black or went back far enough that light couldn't penetrate. It looked like the sort of space where there should be a statue of a saint or Jesus or Mary or something, but it was empty. On the short stone platform in front of it were fingernails and photographs, underwear and hats, stuff that appeared to have been left by previous visitors.

Frank had never known anyone brave enough to actually go to the shrine—until tonight—and he found himself wondering if maybe the people who had come here before were adults. The thought frightened him. He imagined Mr. Christensen or Mr. Wallace or maybe even Chase's mom sneaking out here in the middle of the night to ask for a raise or a baby or a new car.

Johnny's dad got a new car last year.

Frank didn't want to think about it. He focused his attention on Chaz and Paul. What the hell were they doing? Both boys were unbuckling their belts, pulling down their pants and pointing their erect peckers at the shrine. They started stroking themselves.

"Your brother's a homo," Johnny whispered.

Chase elbowed him in the side.

"Ow!"

Frank held his breath, afraid his friend's outburst would give them away, but the older boys were too engrossed in their activity to pay attention. Neither of them spoke. Chaz had placed his flashlight on top of an upside-down garbage can, pointing the beam at that dark featureless alcove, and the light threw the two into clear relief. Frank could see their right arms moving in tandem, a rhythmic back and forth motion as they stroked themselves.

He wanted to go home. It was too dark to see his friends' expressions, but they had to be freaked by this, too. They were out of their depth here.

Suddenly Paul stiffened, and a beat later Chaz did the same. Their arm movements accelerated, reaching a fever pitch, and then stopped. Both boys' heads drooped, as if they were exhausted, and their arms hung limply at their sides.

Something moved out of the dark opening in the middle of the shrine, a small awkwardly waddling creature that looked like a burnt Barbie doll. It had a horrible, powerful stench, the reek of rotting vegetables, and in the middle of its blackened mouth was one single shiny ultra-white tooth. It squeaked when it moved, not the animal squeal of a mouse but more like the mechanical squeak of a rusty door hinge.

Frank had never been so scared in his life. This was something out of a nightmare, only it was far worse than any nightmare he had ever had. The blackened creature stepped directly into the flashlight beam, but that did not render its features any more clear or its appearance any less frightening. It stopped waddling, stood on a pile of clipped fingernails, and its squeaking intensified, speeding up, gaining in volume.

Paul suddenly dropped to his knees, while Chaz backed away in horror. It was as though the burnt feature had spoken to them and they had understood. Chase's brother, still facing the shrine, seemingly unable to look away, continued backing up until he hit a bush and could go no farther. Paul bowed down like a man about to be knighted, like a subject prostrating himself before his king, head and shoulders touching the ground. The figure reached out, caressed his hair, then bent forward, its single-toothed mouth pressing against Paul's ear. The squeaking subsided to a whisper.

And Paul started convulsing.

Only the bottom of the flashlight beam touched him, but it was enough for them to see the spastic vibrations assaulting his body. The burnt creature was still whispering, and beneath the sibilance Frank heard the sickening crunch of bone on stone as Paul's head jerked up and down, slamming repeatedly into the platform, knocking aside panties and baseball caps and photographs and fingernails. Blood black enough to be oil spread out from beneath the boy's smashed face and engulfed the personal items, and Frank suddenly realized that the creature's whispering had turned to hissing laughter.

Chaz ran.

The rest of them followed.

All of them were screaming. Chaz had left his flashlight and Chase hadn't turned his flashlight on, but somehow they got out of the backyard easier and faster than they'd gotten in. They ran through the tangled jungle of dead plants and debris that was the witch's front yard, and then they were on the sidewalk.

"Oh shit!" Frank said, looking ahead. He grabbed the back of Chase's collar, put his right arm out to block Johnny and forced his two friends into Johnny's yard.

His dad was walking Aarfy and was less than a house away!

What the hell was he doing out this late?

Chase's brother had seen him, too, and the older boy ran up shouting, "Mr. Marotta! Mr. Marotta!"

"That's your dad!" Johnny said.

"No shit, Sherlock." Frank ducked behind a camellia bush next to Johnny's front porch and dragged his friends with him. They watched as Chaz explained what had happened, gesticulating wildly. Then he took Aarfy and ran toward Frank's house, while Frank's dad hurried over to the witch's yard.

"Fuck!" Chase said. "Your dad's gonna get killed."

"No he's not!" Frank responded, but he wanted to jump up and leap out of the bushes and yell for his dad to *Stop! Turn around! Stay away from there!* An instinct for survival and self-preservation kept him mute, however, and he told himself that whatever had happened was over and his dad would be fine, and he made himself believe it.

Johnny stood. "I'm going inside. I'm through."

"But we gotta find out what happened to Paul!" Chase said.

"Your brother's going to get help, probably call the police. Frank's dad's over there now. There's nothing else we can do. I'm going to bed and I'm not waking up until the sun's out!"

"I'm going home, too," Frank said.

"Pussies," Chase said, but there was no meaning behind it. He was scared, also. It was his brother's friend who had been killed, but his brother was still alive, and like the rest of them he probably wanted to go home and hide in the safety of his well-lighted house until this night was done.

"Later, guys," Frank said. He hurried back across Johnny's lawn to the sidewalk, looking toward the witch's place, half-hoping to see his dad, but the old man was nowhere in sight and the dilapidated house was completely dark.

The entire street seemed much more threatening than it had earlier this evening, the night not merely a darker version of the day but an entity unto itself. Glancing back periodically at the witch's house—

Why hadn't he shouted out to his dad?

—Frank jogged down the sidewalk toward home, humming a song to himself, trying to keep his fears at bay.

"hello?"

The voice was small, soft, barely audible. It was a girl's voice, and it came from up ahead, from behind the Millers' hedges.

"hello?"

Frank slowed, stopped. He thought for a moment, then walked into the street, making a big detour around the hedges. If something was hiding behind there, waiting for him, ready to jump out at him, he wasn't going to sit still for it and make the attacker's job easy. He walked out to the middle of the circle, then passed by the hedge boundary and looked back toward the Millers'.

It really was a girl.

And she was *naked!*

She was sitting on one of the decorative boulders that the Millers had in their

Southwest-themed yard, and he could see everything! She didn't even seem to care! A streetlight in front of the house shone on her like a spotlight, and he saw her long blond hair, her small pointy breasts, the triangle of hair between her legs.

He felt like he'd died and gone to heaven, and he quickly looked to the right to see if Chase or Johnny were still around— though even if they were, he was not sure he'd invite them over. There was no sign of either of his friends, however, and Frank walked back over the asphalt to the sidewalk, stopping at the edge of the Millers' property, about five feet away from her.

She looked at him. Her eyes, he saw, were large and blue. "hello?" she said in that soft small voice.

"Hi," Frank responded. His own voice sounded much softer than he'd intended, and his throat felt dry.

She stood up from the boulder and walked carefully across the Millers' gravel toward him, the small rocks obviously hurting the soft bottoms of her bare feet. She grimaced as she stepped onto the sidewalk next to him. Her approach was so open and straightforward that he half-expected her to put her arms around his neck and kiss him—

Had Chase been wishing for a naked girl when they were crouched near the shrine? Had his wish been granted?

—but instead she said, "Where am I?"

Frank didn't know how to answer, didn't know what she was asking. "Uh, William Tell Circle," he said.

She nodded, looked around.

"Where are you from?" he asked her.

She shrugged. "I don't know."

"Well, where are your parents?"

She looked at him as if she didn't understand the question. "I don't know," she said finally.

They seemed to have reached the end of their conversation. She apparently had no more questions to ask, and despite the fact that she was a naked babe, maybe *because* she was a naked babe, he was a little freaked by her. He looked down the sidewalk toward his house, wishing he'd never sneaked out tonight. Behind him, though he couldn't see it, he was acutely aware of the dark tangled jungle that was the witch's house.

Where his dad was.

"I...I have to go home," he said.

The girl touched his arm. "My name's Sue," she said. "What's your name?"

He swallowed hard. "Frank," he told her. It was the first time any girl had touched him, let alone a naked girl, and he thought about the story he'd have to tell Chase and Johnny. Once more, he glanced toward their houses to see if they were out and watching what was going on. It was going to be impossible to make them believe this unless they saw it for themselves.

The girl, Sue, took her hand away, letting her fingers trail down his wrist, over the back of his hand.

"I have to go home," he said again, thinking about his dad and prodded by a vague sense of urgency.

She nodded, but when he started walking, she followed him. Like a puppy dog, he thought.

He stopped. She stopped.

He turned and asked the question he'd been wanting to ask since he saw her: "Where are your clothes?"

She smiled. "I don't have any."

"O-Kay." He stretched the word out, in that sarcastic way he'd heard high school kids do.

She kept smiling.

"Look, it's late at night, and I really do have to go home, all right?" He glanced over at the witch's house. No sign of movement. No sign of his father.

"All right," Sue said.

Not only did she follow him, but she took his hand, holding it in hers like they were boyfriend and girlfriend. He wanted to shake her off him, wanted to get the hell away from her. How was he going to explain this to his mom? But he also wanted to keep holding her hand, keep touching her, maybe touch her somewhere *else,* and he was beginning to think that he might be in love with her.

Was she in love with him?

It seemed so.

Together they walked back to his house and up the driveway.

He left her out front, in the patio between the garage and the house, while he went inside. He had a feeling it wasn't a good idea to spring a naked space cadet on his mom without warning her first. Luckily, Sue didn't ask any questions but acceded to his bluntly stated wishes.

His mom was in the family room. Alone, eating an apple and watching an old Harrison Ford movie.

Frank frowned. "Where's Chaz?" he said. "Did you guys call the police?"

"What?"

He knew from his mother's tone of voice that Chaz had never made it here, that she had no idea what had happened. He suddenly felt cold. "Where's Aarfy?" he asked.

"Oh, your dad took him for a walk." She squinted as she looked at him, seeming to notice for the first time that he was dressed and not in pajamas. She put on her Mom voice. "Where have you been?"

"That—" *witch's house,* he'd been about to say, but instead he said, "—lady professor's house. Chase's brother and his friend Paul were going back there to ask for three thousand dollars from the shrine to buy a car, only Paul got killed and Chaz ran into Dad and told him about it and Dad's back there now and Chaz was supposed to bring Aarfy back home and come here and tell you and call the police." It all spilled out in a confusing torrent—and he hadn't even gotten to the naked girl yet—but his mom seemed to understand his story even as she dismissed it.

"Chaz Pittman probably just scared himself—"

"We were there, Mom. We saw it. Me and Chase and Johnny."

"hello?"

Great. Sue wandered into the living room, peeking tentatively around the corner before stepping forward in all her glory. This was all he needed.

"Dad could get killed!" he yelled. "Call the damn police!"

He had never sworn in front of either of his parents before, and that got her attention.

"*What* did you say?" She stood, put her apple down on the table and glared at him.

Frank felt like sobbing with frustration. "Chaz's friend Paul was killed in that woman's backyard. By a little burned monster. I saw it. Dad went back there to check up on it, and I should have stopped him but I didn't, and now he might get killed, too." He did start to cry. "Call the police."

Some of his fear must have translated because now anger and worry were battling it out on his mother's face, and she strode past the naked girl, opened the front door and scanned the street. "Gil?" she called. There was no answer, and she shouted his name again, louder. "Gil!"

"Call 'em," Frank said, crying.

She ran into the kitchen, where the nearest phone was, and he returned to the living room, slumping down gratefully in her chair. On TV, Harrison Ford was hiding in a barn from some bad guys who were trying to kill him. How nice that would be, he thought. You could get away from a person. You could hide, you could fight, you could win. But the thing that came out of that shrine...

He sat up suddenly. Where was Sue? She'd been standing there only a few minutes ago, and he'd expected her to follow him into the room, thought she'd probably sit herself down right next to him. And where was his mom? She should have been back in here by now. Or at least he should have been able to hear her voice. He picked up the remote control, pressed the Mute button.

The house was silent.

No.

Frank jumped up and ran to the kitchen. He should have sneaked over, should have approached carefully, but the last thing he was thinking of was his own safety—he wanted to know if his mom was okay, and he wanted to know *now*—and he dashed through the entryway and swung around the side of the refrigerator until he could see the entire room.

His mom was not okay. She was lying on the floor just below the wall phone, the receiver dangling above her head, spinning on its spiral cord. Her eyes were open, staring at nothing, and blood dripped from her mouth in a thick mucus-like strand. There was blood on her back, too, deep animal-like scratches. Frank could see her back because Sue had ripped his mother's shirt off. The naked girl was kneeling on the floor behind her, trying to pull down her pants, humming a nursery-rhyme ditty that sounded suspiciously like *Here We Go 'Round the Mulberry Bush*. The girl's chest and stomach were smeared with blood, though there didn't appear to be a scratch on her.

Frank stood there for a moment, frozen, torn between wanting to rush at the little bitch, beat the shit out of her, give his mom mouth-to-mouth and save her life, and wanting to turn tail and run like hell away from that monster.

Fear won out. His mom's eyes were open, unblinking; it was obvious that she was dead and there was nothing he could do to bring her back. Sue had somehow murdered her in—what? four minutes?—and unless he got out of here quick, she'd be doing the same to him.

So he ran back out of the kitchen, through the entryway, out the front door, down the driveway and onto the sidewalk. He glanced quickly behind him, but Sue wasn't following, and he looked over at the witch's house. As he'd feared, as he'd known, there was no sign of his dad.

Frank dashed next door to the Boykins' house, but changed his mind at the last minute and ran across their lawn to the Millers', leaping the small line of rose bushes in between. The Boykins' porch light was on, but he'd seen when he got closer that there was no light in their living room or kitchen, and he figured they were probably asleep. They were old, went to bed early, and he didn't want to spend ten minutes ringing their bell and pounding on their door while he waited for them to open up.

He might not have ten minutes.

That was the thought in the forefront of his mind, and he saw again his mom's dead staring eyes, her drool of thick blood, the deep scratches on her bare back.

The Millers' house was dark, too, and he swerved up their driveway and back onto the sidewalk, running next door. He knew he could just knock on Johnny's bedroom window and get his friend's attention, so he bypassed the front stoop and ran around the side of the house, rapping both fists on the windowglass. "Open up!" he yelled. "Hurry!" He looked over his shoulder, expecting to see Sue coming toward him, arms outstretched, covered in his mom's blood, but the coast was clear.

"Johnny!" he called.

The drapes did not part, no light shone between the cracks.

Frank kept pounding, his stomach sinking a little. "Johnny!"

No noise, no light.

He stopped rapping on the window and pressed his face against the glass, trying in vain to see something through the narrow breach where the curtains met. Behind him was the Millers' bedroom window. The two homes were close together, and he half-hoped that his pounding and shouting had woken up either Mr. or Mrs. Miller, but when he looked over there, the house was dark.

He'd found Sue in front of the Millers' home.

Johnny's side yard suddenly didn't seem quite so safe. But this was his friend's place. He knew this house, knew these people, and he ran into the backyard, ready to take one last chance and pound the shit out of Johnny's parents' bedroom window.

Their window was open, though, as were their drapes. The light was off in the room, but a back porch lamp was on, and by that indirect illumination he could see their bodies naked and strewn across the blood-spattered bed. Between them was another naked form, a girl, a blond girl. It wasn't Sue, but there was definitely a resemblance, and she was on all fours, licking blood off Johnny's dad's face. He heard the lapping of the girl's tongue, smelled the horrid heavy stink of death, and he immediately started puking. Instinct and decorum dictated that he should bend over and remain in place until he finished regurgitating the contents of his stomach, but his brain knew that to do so would mean almost certain death and overrode that impulse. Still throwing up, the vomit splashing over his shirtfront and onto the ground, Frank fled, running back around the side yard the way he'd come.

Johnny's parents were dead.

That meant Johnny was dead, too.

He wanted to scream in terror, wanted to run straight down the street and not stop running until he hit the police station two miles away, but his dad was still at the witch's house, and though he doubted there was anything he could do to save his father if he was really in trouble, Frank knew he had to try. He was more frightened than he had ever been in his life, but he hurried without hesitation down the sidewalk toward the lightless black space that was the professor's yard. He was drawing on strength he didn't even know he possessed, and he thought it was probably like the resolve that sent firemen into burning buildings, that made soldiers run through gunfire to save their buddies in time of war.

He thought about those naked girls as he ran. What were they? They had something to do with the shrine, of that he was sure, but why were they going around the neighborhood killing people?

Had they gotten Chaz and Aarfy?

He'd forgotten about Chase's brother and the dog until now, and he wished he hadn't remembered. The two of them had obviously disappeared somewhere between the spot where they'd left his dad, and his home, where they were supposed to be headed. Even though that was only four houses away.

He kept running, acutely aware that at any second *he* might be attacked, that one of the naked girls or...something else might suddenly take him out and make him disappear. He glanced over at Chase's home, saw the porch light on, saw the flickering blue light of a television through the sheer curtains. Everything looked normal. But Chaz had disappeared, and for all Frank knew Chase and his parents lay slaughtered inside. He looked back at Johnny's place, at the Millers', at his own. The entire street looked normal, actually, a typical night in a typical suburban neighborhood, and it was scary how deceptive appearances could be.

Then he was running across the dark front yard of the witch's house for the second time this night, and though his heart was pounding with terror, though his feet wanted to veer back toward the street, he turned around the side of the building and ran past the lawnmower, the washing machine, the tree stump, the buckets, into the backyard.

The moon was up now, and he could see better than he could before, but the back-yard still seemed darker, filled with horrors he could not see and not imagine. He re-membered that burnt waddling doll-like thing and the terrible squeaking it made, and his blood felt like ice water. He could not continue to run back here, it was too crowded. He stopped, looked around. He didn't want to draw attention to himself, didn't want anyone or any*thing* to know he was here, but he had to find his father. "Dad!" he called out, searching the dark-ness for signs of movement. "Dad!"

As he'd expected, as he'd feared, there was no answer, but he refused to give up, refused to let himself believe that his dad was dead.

He pressed on, moved farther into the backyard. "Dad!" he called, but he did not shout as loudly this time.

"Dad?" Volume falling.

"Dad." A low rough whisper.

Something about this place discour-aged loudness, intimidated him into silence. He didn't want to go anywhere near the shrine, but he knew that was exactly where he needed to go if he really wanted to know what had happened to his father. He walked around a tangled dead stickerbush, then down the narrow path that he seemed to remember leading to the shrine.

"Dad," he said—

—and tripped over something in the dirt.

There wasn't time to break his fall. He tumbled forward, sprawling, and his forehead hit something soft and smelly that he thought was a rotten watermelon. One hand and arm scraped the hard dirt ground while the other twisted beneath him but luckily did not break. His knees and legs fell on what felt like a sack of sand, and he immediately pulled himself forward, lurching to his feet.

It wasn't a sack of sand. It was a dead body.

It was Chase.

He was on his back, facing up. His face had been chewed on, and over his forehead and what remained of his cheeks scurried big black beetles that in the moonlight appeared to be the same shade of pitch as the burnt creature in the shrine.

Frank screamed once, an instinctive reaction of shock and horror, but he immediately stopped and shut up. Whatever did this was still out there, and he couldn't let it know he was here, couldn't give away his location.

Ahead was the shrine, but he could not continue on. He was in way over his head here, and it was time to call in the cops. For all he knew, everyone in the neighborhood was dead, so he couldn't count on being able to rouse a neighbor. He didn't even want to take a chance with someone on the next street over. He would go to the Arco station over on Washington. Even if the gas station was closed, it had a pay phone out front, and he was pretty sure you could dial 911 from a pay phone without having to put in money. If not, there was a Circle K farther down that was open twenty-four hours.

He stepped carefully over Chase's body, not looking down, then hurried up the path the way he'd come.

A light went on in the house.

Frank ducked behind a half-collapsed pile of old bricks, trying to not even breathe, afraid the witch would know he was here and come after him. He didn't know for sure that the light had been turned on by the professor or that she was really a witch or that she had anything to do with what had gone on tonight, but he was not willing to take that chance, and he crouched lower. Spiderwebs tickled his face and arms—he even thought he felt the quick scurrying legs of the spider itself on the back of his wrist—but he remained in place, silent, un-moving, hoping and praying that the light would go off and she would go away.

The light did not go off. Another light went on. And a creaky door opened.

"I'm scared."

The girl's voice was right next to him, soft and frightened, and his heart started thumping hard. *Sue,* he thought. But it wasn't Sue. This girl was dark-haired and dressed, wearing what looked like a Catholic school uniform: white blouse, blue skirt. She also looked vaguely familiar, and Frank thought that he had seen her before at the library or the park or the grocery store.

Had she been there the whole time? It was possible, but he had the feeling that she had crept over here from somewhere else, somewhere close, her own hiding place.

"I'm scared."

"Shhh," he told her, and the two of them remained quiet, waiting, but there was no further sound, no indication that anyone had come out of the house into the backyard.

His right leg was starting to cramp, and his left wrist still hurt from where he'd fallen on it. He shifted position until he was facing the girl and no longer had to turn his head to see her. Tears were streaming down her cheeks, shiny like snail trails in the moonlight.

"What are you doing here?" he whispered.

She'd been sobbing quietly, but she pulled herself together, sniffled. "I just came here with two friends of mine. I didn't even want to. They wanted to. They were going to…ask the shrine for…something. But they're gone. I think they're dead."

Frank ignored the hair bristling on his arms. "What makes you think that?"

"There was this little burned doll. It was alive. And it…it…" She started sobbing again.

"What's your name?" He thought if he could distract her, maybe she'd stop crying and start talking and he'd be able to find out some information.

"Cass," she said.

"I'm Frank."

They were still whispering, still very much afraid of being overheard and found out, and the whispering made everything seem so much more…intimate. It was a strange word to be using in such a time and place, but that's how he felt. He'd never been so near to a girl before—

except Sue

—and despite the circumstances, or maybe because of them, there was something strangely exciting and exhilarating about their close quarters conversation.

"I go to John Adams," he said.

She wiped her eyes, her nose. "Me, too."

"I thought you looked familiar. What grade are you?"

"Seventh."

"I'm in eighth." Frank looked over her shoulder. He couldn't see all of the house through the bushes, but he could see that both lights were still on. He heard no one else out here, though, no other sounds save their own breathing and whispers.

He didn't know what else to say, and she obviously didn't feel like talking, so they crouched there in silence. Cass shifted position, her fingers accidentally brushing the back of his hand, a touch that felt electric. He wanted to reach out, take her hand in his, hold it.

He shouldn't be thinking of her like this. His mom had been killed, his dad was probably dead, Chase's body was lying on the ground less than five feet away, Johnny and his parents had been murdered, and *her* friends were missing and probably dead. What the hell was wrong with him?

The door of the house creaked again—someone coming out? someone going back in?—and they both froze. Once more, there were no other sounds, no sign of activity, but they remained in place for a long time afterward, not speaking, afraid to move.

Cass was no longer crying, no longer sniffling, and after what seemed like an hour of doing absolutely nothing but the minimum amount of breathing necessary to stay alive, Frank forced himself to relax a little. "Hey," he whispered.

"Hey," she said back.

"So what happened to your friends? Did you see it?"

Silence. At first he thought she wasn't going to answer, then finally she said softly, "I saw part of it."

When it became clear that she wasn't going to say any more, he decided to try a different tack. "What were they going to ask for?"

"I don't know," she said quickly, embarrassed.

"Come on."

"What were *your* friends going to ask for?"

"I asked you first."

Even in the blue illumination of the moonlight, he thought he could see her redden. "A guy."

Frank laughed. It was the first funny thing he had heard all night. She punched his shoulder. "So? What about you?"

"Two of us were just along for the ride. But our friend—

Chase

—was going to ask for—" Now it was his turn to redden. "—a girl."

"Looks like we both got our wish, huh?"

He couldn't see her face, she'd leaned back into the shadow, and he wasn't sure how to take that. In his mind, she'd been smiling sadly, but maybe she had a different kind of expression on her face. Against his

will, he felt himself responding, felt a stir-
ring in his lap.

Again? Jesus. His mom was dead, his
friends were dead, half the neighborhood
was dead, and his dad was missing. How
could he even think about such a thing at a
time like this?

"Maybe we should try to get out of
here," he suggested. "Try to get some help."

She nodded.

"You think we can make it? You think
anyone's out there?"

"Stay there. I'll check." She suddenly
stood up to take a look around, and he
could see up her skirt.

She wasn't wearing any underwear.

Now he was completely aroused. It was
too dark to see anything clearly, anything
specific, but he saw darkness, saw hair, and
it was the most exciting sight he had ever
laid eyes on.

She quickly crouched back down again.
"Let's wait a minute," she told him.

Frank looked at her, not sure if she was
genuinely worried that they might not make

it out of the witch's backyard or if she merely wanted to remain here and spend more time with him. Did she know he could see up her skirt? Had she wanted him to look?

As if in answer, she moved a little closer. "I took off my underwear before I left the house," she said. "We all did."

He looked at her, saying nothing.

She knew he'd seen, she'd wanted him to see.

"We heard you and your friends talking," she admitted. "You were wondering what it would taste like to…to…you know." She glanced shyly, nervously licked her lips. "Are you still curious?"

He didn't know what to say, didn't know how to respond. This was like a porno book. Or one of Chase's lies about his brother.

"It's okay if you—" she said quickly.

He swallowed hard. "Yes," he managed to croak out.

Now it was her turn to be tongue-tied.

"I didn't mean…I wasn't trying to…" He let the thought trail off, not sure how to finish it.

Cass took a deep breath. "I wouldn't mind if you...you know...did that."

They looked at each other, both unsure of what to say next or how to proceed. He was the boy, he supposed he should be the one to take the initiative, so he reached up tentatively, put his arms around her waist, drawing her closer. She didn't object, and slowly, he moved his head up under her skirt.

He kissed her there, stuck out his tongue, pressed it in.

She couldn't have heard them talking, he realized. They hadn't talked about that here. They'd talked about it in Chase's house earlier in the afternoon.

His skin erupted in goosebumps.

She was one of them.

He should have known it. Nothing about this made any sense, scenes like this just didn't happen in real life, and it was his own fault that he fell for it, that he went along with it. His friends and family were dead, and here he was indulging in some

Penthouse Forum fantasy in the filthy back-yard of a witch.

But why hadn't she killed him yet? What did she want? What was she waiting for?

He couldn't let her know what he knew. Surprise was his only chance. So he wiggled his tongue around the area, kept licking. She'd been talking, saying something, and though he hadn't been paying attention, he noticed now that she was no longer saying words. Her voice had turned into a me-chanical squeak, the same sort of noise that burned thing in the shrine had made. From the direction of the shrine came a pound-ing, an echoing boom that superceded all other sound.

It was now or never.

He tried to pull away, tried to slowly and unobtrusively move back, in preparation for a mad dash to get the hell out of here... but he could not. His lips were sealed to her genitals, and he felt something *moving* over his lips, creeping outward over the skin of his cheeks and chin and up by his nostrils. It was like a new skin was growing, fusing the two of them together, joining his lips to her vagina.

He and his friends would've joked about this, would've laughed if they'd read about it or heard it from someone else. "The dude musta died with a smile on his face," he could imagine Chase saying. But it was real, it was here, and there was nothing funny about it.

He tried to yank his head away, but that produced only a sharp sensation of pain as the movement threatened to pull off the skin from the lower half of his face. He started punching her in the stomach as hard as he could, hoping it would get her to release him, wondering even as he did so whether she had any control of what was going on between her legs.

The punches seemed to have no effect, and that creeping skin was starting to cover up his nostrils, cutting off his air, so he felt blindly around until his fingers curled around one of the piled bricks. He gripped it tightly, then brought it up and slammed it against her side. There was no reaction, no response, not even any blood. The brick hit her skin and did no damage. She was squeaking loudly now, like a rusted train being pulled down unused tracks, and her wet skin sealed shut his nostrils, fusing with his face, and he knew that he was about to die.

Her skin tightened on his own, squeezing his head. Cartilage in his nose broke, splintered into fragments. The bones in his cheek shattered. He swallowed two teeth that popped out, held two others loose in his mouth. He was getting weak from the lack of oxygen. He dropped the brick, unable to hold it any longer, and his arms and legs dangled loosely, uselessly, as though his body were already dead and only his brain was still alive. He was being held up, suspended by their fused skin. And then...

And then...

He was let go. The skin of his face was his skin again, he was no longer connected to her, and he fell back onto the ground, the back of his head hitting the brick that he'd dropped. He felt a warm gush of blood. He wanted to sit up, wanted to roll away, but he could not move. He was too weak, and he realized with horror that although he was free from her, he had not been saved. He had been too hurt, had been without oxygen for too long, was losing too much blood. He was still dying, and unless he got to a hospital pretty damn quick, he was not going to make it.

Dad?

He could barely see, could not smell at all, and his right ear was filled with blood, making all sound muffled, but he was filled with the certainty that his father was here, nearby, and that he was okay, that he had not been harmed. A sense of relief flooded over him, and for the first time since that burned thing had killed Paul, he had the feeling that everything was going to be all right.

Above him, Cass was still standing, and as he watched she faded away, disappearing into the shadows, into the night, the most devastating expression on her face that he had ever seen, a look not only of the purest physical agony but of a knowledge so horrible that he could not even imagine what it might be.

He was fading himself, dying, his eyelids getting heavier, his vision more blurry, his strength ebbing. He thought he heard his father's voice, somewhere close, saying "Take that" and he wanted to call out, tried to call out, knowing that if he could get his father's attention, if his dad could just find him and speed him over to the hospital, all would be well.

But no sound emerged from his mouth, and he found that he could not even move his lips.

His eyes were completely closed now, permanently shut, and he knew finally and with certainty that he was not going to make it. He heard his dad's voice fading away, heard everything fading away. On his tongue, he could still taste the girl, still taste her sex.

It did taste like honey, he thought.

It did.

It did.

GIL

I don't know why I didn't go to work. I don't know what made me stay home. Part of it was that I hated the swing shift. I'd been transferred over from graveyard the week before, and while most people think graveyard's a bitch, it's a cakewalk compared to swing. Now, I've never been one of those guys to use sick days to attend my kid's baseball game or band concert or school play. Hell, I don't even use them when I'm really sick. But somehow the prospect of another night of swing, combined with the fact that it was Friday and yesterday I'd been denied a vacation in October that corresponded with Lynn's...well, let's just say that the decision to play hooky wasn't a tough one to make.

I called the plant and told them I wouldn't be coming in. Luckily, I didn't have to talk to a real person. I don't think I could've gone through with it if I did; I'm not a very good liar. But I got Human Resources' answering machine—maybe a lot of other people were calling in sick, too—and I quickly left my message and then took the phone off the hook so they wouldn't be able to call me back.

Home free.

Even though it wasn't a school night, Lynn made Frank go to bed at eight. He'd done something he wasn't supposed to before dinner, and while she'd told me about it, I'd only half been paying attention and didn't really know what it was. Still, I automatically supported her, and when he appealed to me for clemency, I said, "You heard your mother."

Afterward, the two of us sat on the couch in the living room, snuggling together, watching TV, and it was just like the old times before we had Frank. I was even thinking that I might get lucky. Her pants were unbuttoned, the way they often were after a full dinner, and when I slipped my hand inside them she didn't object like she usually did and push me away, looking over her shoulder to make sure Frank wasn't creeping up on us. She let my hand stay there, my fingers pressed against her crotch, and it was nice.

Then Aarfy started barking. That stupid dog was howling up a storm, desperate to go out, and I realized that no one had taken him for a walk after dinner. I'd thought it was Frank's turn; he'd obviously thought it was mine, so even though it was late, already after nine, I got up off the couch, leashed him up and took him once around the block.

We were almost home when it happened. Aarfy was making one last pit stop at the fire hydrant in front of the Millers' when I heard screams. It sounded like a bunch of kids, but when I looked up I saw only one guy running toward me.

"Mr. Marotta! Mr. Marotta!"

It was one of the Pittman kids, the older one (I could never remember his name), speeding down the sidewalk, waving his arms. There was panic in his voice, and when he got closer I could see that his shirt was torn. There was a big dark stain on it, and while I didn't know what it was, my first thought was: *blood*.

Then he reached me, and I saw that it was one of those shirts that was supposed to be torn and the dark stain was a picture of a monster or something. Still, he was panicked, terrified, and I held up my hand. "Slow down there, bud, slow down. What seems to be the problem?"

I thought it might be a dog that got hit by a car, or maybe even that his mom had a heart attack or had been beaten by his dad. But I wasn't prepared for the story he told me. It came in confused bits and pieces. He was too rattled to think straight, but I was able to jigsaw fit his frightened disjointed utterances, and what he said seemed unbelievable. He and his friend Paul had snuck into the backyard of the pigsty next to Ed Christensen's house because there was supposed to be a shrine hidden there that could grant wishes if you approached it in the right way and were willing to pay the price it asked. They hadn't even gotten around to asking, though, when a monster that looked like a burned-up doll came creeping out of a hole in the middle of the shrine. The Pittman kid was afraid of it, but his friend Paul had a weird reaction and bowed down before it like he was worshiping a god. Then the monster touched Paul and whispered in his ear, and he started having some sort of spastic fit, slamming his own head down on the ground until he'd split it open and was dead.

I wasn't sure how much of this I actually believed, but I believe it more than I usually would have just because of the kid's panic. He was terrified, he'd seen something that scared the living shit out of him, and whether he'd added or embellished or exaggerated, I thought the crux of his story was true. Something bad had happened in the backyard of that house and now his friend was dead.

I'd never seen the woman who lived in the house at the end of the cul de sac. In fact, I only knew that a woman lived there because Ed had told me about her, although I'm not sure he'd ever seen her either. She was supposed to be a teacher at the JC, some sort of physics or philosophy professor. Her house was a mess, the front yard a jungle of dead trees and overgrown weeds, the backyard even worse, and Ed and Tony and some of the other neighborhood neatniks had circulated a petition to have the city crack down on what they said were health code violations. I'd been tempted not to sign it just on general principles. A person's house wasn't a democracy. Neighbors didn't get to vote on how it looked. It was a dictatorship. And the owner had the complete and total right to do whatever he wanted with his house and his land.

Or hers.

But the truth was that the damn place smelled like a catbox. Santa Ana winds hit just right, and the foul stench of that yard even made it over to my house. I could imagine what it was like for Ed and Tony. Not to mention the fact that Frank sometimes played over at his friend Johnny's house next door. I didn't like the idea of my boy being exposed to germs and rats and who-knows-what-all over there.

So I'd signed the petition, but nothing came of it. Ed said the city sent someone down, some inspector, but that the old lady was never home. He was trying to get them to go to the junior college and hit her up where she worked, serve her with a subpoena or some sort of notice ordering her to clean up her yard, but they weren't willing to go that far. So there it sat.

I'd never heard of this shrine before, and I don't know why I believe it was really there, but I did. I remembered neighborhood legends and secrets from when I was a kid, things that parents didn't know existed but that we'd seen or sometimes even built with our own hands. There was a whole separate world that parents didn't know about, and I'm sure the same thing was true today.

Aarfy was barking, straining at his leash, getting anxious. "Here," I said to the Pittman boy, handing him the leash. "Take my dog home. Tell my wife what happened, and call 911. I'm going to go over there and check—"

"Don't, Mr. Marotta! That monster's still there! It's small but it's...Jesus Christ! I've never seen anything like it!"

The monster was the one part of his story I definitely didn't believe.

"Look, I'll be fine. Get to my house, tell my wife, call 911. I'm going over there now." What had just occurred to me was that his friend Paul might still be alive and in need of emergency medical attention. I didn't know CPR, not exactly, but I'd seen it in movies and on TV and figured I knew enough to keep the kid alive until police or paramedics came by.

The boy stood there stupidly, holding on to the leash.

"Go!" I told him.

He ran off toward my house, Aarfy leading the way, and I hurried away in the opposite direction. All the homes on the circle had backlit curtains and porch lights on, but the professor's house was totally dark. With the bushy trees around and behind it, all individual features obscured, it looked like a giant amoeba, like The Blob or something, but I pushed that thought away. I didn't want to let that kid's fear and paranoia get to me, and the last thing I needed to do was start thinking about monster movies.

I thought of knocking on the door first, but it looked pretty unlikely that the professor was home, so I cut across her driveway and ran by her front window toward the side of the house, nearly tripping over a rock or some other hard object half-buried in the ground.

I slowed down when I reached the side yard. It was just too damn dirty and crowded to go running through. I didn't want to slam my shin against something or cut myself on a rusty piece of metal. Besides, I was almost out of breath just from running across the street to get here.

I walked carefully through the rubbish and into the backyard. This was a corner lot—if there could be corner lots on a circle—and was bigger than most of the other backyards. Bigger than mine, that's for sure.

It was also a bona fide health hazard, filled with more junk and garbage than I had ever seen before. It looked like a fucking dump. Not "dump" as in ratty place but "dump" as in landfill. It literally looked like four or five garbage trucks had tilted their backs over her fence and deposited all their contents on her dead lawn. There were a lot of trees and bushes here, but there were even more garbage cans and moldy cardboard boxes and pieces of rusted scrap metal. I walked past a garage door opener propped against a drawerless wooden dresser, the hood of a white car piled high with broken clay pots and bags of charcoal.

I made my way down a narrow path through the debris. There, between a collapsed playhouse and a sticker bush that appeared to have overgrown a rotted woodpile, was the shrine. I knew what it was immediately, and the sight of it sent a shiver through my bones. It was the creepiest thing I'd ever seen, and I wished I'd thought to bring a flashlight. Hell, I wished I'd stopped by the Christensens' house, gotten Ed off his dead ass and made him come back here with me. I might be an adult, but this place was spooky, and it wouldn't hurt to have someone else along for the ride.

The shrine was a Catholic-looking adobe thing, like one of those old altars in a Mexican village or something. But there was no saint in its alcove, only a black empty space. It wasn't like the statue of a saint had been stolen or anything, it was more like that black space itself was the thing being worshiped. I can't explain it any better than that, but that's how I felt and it scared me.

There was no dead body, though, no little fire-roasted monster, nothing that would indicate that the Pittman boy (what *was* his name?) had been telling the truth. I'm not sure why I thought it would be otherwise, but I'd honestly expected to find the dead corpse of a teenager laying there and some sort of doll-sized monster eating his flesh.

This place encouraged that kind of thinking.

I turned to look back at the house. It occurred to me that the woman who lived there might not know about the shrine. Her yard was so overgrown, was so densely packed with crap, that someone could hide or even live in it without her knowing. So maybe she didn't know it was back here, maybe someone else had snuck into this fucking pigsty and set up this altar for… what? Witchcraft? To perform satanic services?

Whatever it was, it was nasty, wrong, and even if there was nothing here now, I knew the Pittman kid was telling the truth. His friend *had* died in this spot. I didn't know where the body was now, but it had been here earlier. I was sure of that.

I took a step forward. No one had built this thing recently. It was old. It had been here a long time. I bent down and saw underpants and caps and photos. People had been coming here for years, making pilgrimages to this place. But who? Neighborhood children? The thought terrified me. Had Frank been here? Did he know about this place? Was he involved in a cult or some sort of *River's Edge* thing? I didn't think so, but you could never tell. Parents were always the last people in the world to find out what their kids were really like. I *did* know that Lynn and I kept a close watch on what he did and monitored him pretty closely. He wasn't allowed out at night unless we knew exactly where he was going and with whom. I didn't know what had happened here tonight, but thank God Frank was home right now, in bed, not roaming around like the Pittman kid and his friend.

I looked closer. There were also little white snippets of stuff that looked like fingernails and beneath the fingernails a folded piece of paper that looked familiar—the petition we'd signed to have the health department investigate this place.

I didn't like that. As far as I know, Ed had sent the petition to the city and had kept the only copy for himself. What it was doing here was a mystery. Although since the Pittman boy had said they'd come out here tonight to ask the shrine for money, I couldn't help but think that someone had left the petition here and asked the shrine for something else. What that something else could be, I had no idea.

An icy cold passed through me.

I stood, glanced around the darkness. There was no reason for me to stay. I'd checked what I'd come to check and nothing was there. No dead body, no monster. Now I was trespassing pure and simple. But the certainty that something very bad *had* happened here, all appearances to the contrary, made me decide that I needed to confront the woman who owned the house. Either she had no clue what was going on in her backyard and needed to be told, or she did know and needed to be questioned. Whatever the case, I knew I had to talk to her.

I walked away from the shrine without looking behind me, and made my way back down the path and through the side yard, then across the dead lawn to the front porch. I knocked on the door, waited, knocked on the door, waited, knocked, waited. I must have done this for five full minutes, but there was no answer and I heard no noise from inside the home. A car was in the driveway, an old Ford Torino, and though she could have walked somewhere, could have gone someplace in someone else's car, I didn't think that was the case. She was in there. And she might be in trouble.

I felt suspicious and more than a little scared, and a practical part of me said to get my ass home and call the cops. But another part of me said the Pittman kid had already called cops, who would be here shortly, and they could rescue me if I failed to rescue the professor.

After only a moment's hesitation, I walked around back again and then up the rickety wooden steps that led to a screened-in porch. Not only was the door unlocked, it was open, and a primitive superstitious part of my brain thought that it looked like someone or something was inviting me in. I thought about walking back down the stairs and rooting through that trashy yard for a pipe or some sort of weapon, but I was already at the top and decided to just go in.

The porch was as filthy as the backyard, piled high with old furniture and boxes. "Hello?" I called out. "Anybody home?"

If anybody was, they weren't talking, so I walked a little ways down the porch to where the door to the house itself was. This door was open, too, and the hair on the back of my neck prickled. I almost turned around then and there, but some mule-headed bit of stubbornness refused to let me be frightened off like a nervous little girl, and instead of leaving I stepped into the darkened house.

"Hello?" I called.

There was no answer, and I felt around on the wall next to me for a light switch. I found one and flipped it on.

I didn't know where in the house I thought I was. Some sort of foyer, I suppose. Or a laundry room. I was in a bedroom, though. It was empty, but the bed looked like it had been slept in recently—or else it always looked that way because the professor never made it. That I could never believe. The bedroom was as messy as the porch, with books and newspapers strewn all over the hardwood floor, thick black strings of cobwebs that had collapsed in on themselves hanging from the stucco ceiling. The room smelled of must, dust, old sweat and dried urine, and hanging over an antique chair with ripped upholstery was a nightgown stained with fresh blood.

I wished I had brought a weapon, but it was too late now, and I stuck my hand in my pocket, grabbed my keys and held them in my fist for a makeshift set of brass knuckles. I walked into the next room, another bedroom.

And there she was, sitting in front of a vanity mirror, combing her hair.

"Oh Jesus," I said, and my voice was a whisper that felt like it was going to turn into a scream. "Oh Jesus."

The fat woman's skin was transparent. I remembered hearing a story from a guy at the plant that in pre-war Vietnam, the upper class used to breed rats, force feeding them nothing but ginger root. They'd do this for several generations, and somewhere down the line, when the female rats gave birth, the babies would be transparent and the Vietnamese would eat them as a delicacy because of the subtle ginger flavor that permeated their meat. That's what this reminded me of. Only this was a person not a rat, and I was pretty sure that she had not been born this way; she'd *become* this way.

It was the professor, I assumed, and from the books piled on the bed, it looked like she was a philosophy not physics instructor. I don't know why I noticed that; it had nothing to do with anything.

She was still seated in front of her vanity, but she'd turned away from the mirror and was staring at me. There was a sly smile on her lips, and I could see the white fat of her cheeks through her clear skin, the orangish muscles that worked her mouth. "Which one are you?" she said.

I turned tail and ran. It would have been shorter, probably, to continue on through the house and speed out the front door, but I had no idea what awaited me in other rooms, and my sole thought was to get the hell out of there as quickly as possible. I ran back through that first bedroom, down the length of porch, then leaped the steps and hauled ass around the corner of the house.

I ran next door to Ed's. I thought about going home to call the cops, but I didn't want to upset Lynn any more than she was already or let Frank know anything about this at all, so I opted for Ed's instead. I guess I could've gone to the Pittmans' house and gotten Bill to come with us—it was his kid who'd started this, after all—but I didn't know Bill Pittman that well and didn't like him much and, to be honest, didn't think he'd be much help. He was kind of a dilfy little guy, a scrawny wannabe redneck who was drunk more often than not, and I doubted he'd bring much to the table. Ed, though, was an ex-Marine, a big strapping guy, and while he worked now as a salesman for a drug company, there was still nothing soft about him. He was a good man and a good friend, and while he was a little anal retentive sometimes and a little too by-the-book, he was exactly the type of person I'd want watching my back if I got in a jam.

Ed and his wife were night owls, and I was glad to see that their front door was open. That meant they hadn't gone to sleep yet. But my relief lasted only a few seconds. Because when I reached the screen door, I knew something was wrong immediately. Ed made sure his wife kept their home spotless, but I could see through the screen that the living room was a mess. It looked like a tornado had torn through there.

It looked like the professor's house.

With a sinking feeling in my gut, I opened the door and walked in.

They were on the couch in front of the television, Ed and Judy, and they'd been burned beyond recognition. If it weren't for the fact that they were sitting in their own house on their own sofa and Ed was nearly a foot taller than his wife, I would have had no idea who they were. Their clothes and hair were gone, their faces little more than charred skulls, their bodies blackened bone.

The couch itself was not singed, only the bodies, and it looked like they had been killed elsewhere and posed there. I thought of what the Pittman kid had told me about the little burned monster at the shrine, and I knew this was connected. It made no sense, at least not to me, but somehow it did to someone somewhere, and though these were the bodies of my friends, I kept waiting for them to move and start coming after me.

I felt overwhelmed, not knowing what to do or where to turn. Where were the police? Shouldn't they have been here by now? I glanced at the television set, thought of how I'd left Lynn sitting on the couch, watching a movie. What if something had gotten into my own house, what if something had happened to Lynn or Frank?

I turned, started back out, and saw through the screen a slim shape leaning against the wall at the edge of Ed's garage, a silhouette of cascading hair.

Lynn?

I opened the screen, and the figure walked casually around the edge of the garage toward me.

The hair was Lynn's, but the long thin face beneath it was like nothing I had ever seen. Huge eyebrows jutting across sleepy baggy eyes, and strange lumps protruded from the skin of the cheeks and forehead. The mouth was open but not smiling, revealing stained rectangular teeth behind an oversized upper lip.

But it was the way this creature walked that scared the living fuck out of me. Because it wasn't marching purposefully toward me, wasn't trying to chase me and catch me. It simply was strolling over. As though it knew me. As though we were friends.

I didn't know what it was and didn't want to know. Ed's garage and house were close together, only a couple of steps apart, and the thing was already at the doorway. There was no way I'd be able to get by it. I slammed the front door shut, locked it and ran through the house to the back door. I was in the laundry room when I heard the front door unlock, open and close and the sound of casual footsteps on the hardwood floor of the living room.

Ed and Judy had triple-locked the back door—knob, deadbolt, chain—and it took me a moment to get them all unlatched. Then I was outside and flying. I ran around the dark side of the house, terrified and out of breath, sure that at any second that long-haired travesty of a woman was going to grab me. But nothing did, and I made it safely around the front. I looked across the circle at my house, saw Lynn standing in the open doorway, looking through our screen, as though investigating a noise she'd heard outside.

Or was it Lynn?

Of course it was. Yes, this was a silhouette, too, but I couldn't be fooled twice. I knew my own wife, goddamn it. I was about to shout out to her that she should close the door, lock it and stay inside, when she did exactly that. In the stillness of the neighborhood, I heard the door slam, and a feeling of relief washed over me. She was safe, she was fine.

But for how long?

I was on the sidewalk now and was going to run home and call the cops, but I thought about that long-haired thing following me and I didn't dare let it know where I lived. I had no idea what it was or what it could do, and I wanted to keep it as far away from my family as possible. I looked over my shoulder at the side of the house, but it was still not there, still not coming.

It would be, though.

At its own pace.

In its own way.

It was the shrine that was at the center of all this. I had no idea if it was sitting on some sacred spot and getting its energy from that, or if it had been granted power from some sort of spell, or even if it had been built in such a way that its architecture made it what it was. But I knew it had to be destroyed, knew that if all this was going to stop, I would have to demolish it.

I suddenly thought of a plan.

My friend was coming around the corner, still sauntering in that relaxed unhurried manner. She was far enough away that I couldn't see the specifics of her strange and terrible face, but I'd seen it once and that was enough. I'd never forget it, and when I saw that long cascading hair, my flesh erupted in goosebumps. My gut instinct was to run, to get as far away from her as quickly as possible, but I needed tools, needed weapons, and I ran up the driveway to the garage.

For once, I was grateful for Ed's Felix Unger tendencies. In my own garage, I usually had to dig around for ten minutes to find the tools I needed, but Ed kept everything neatly organized. I had no problem picking out an ax, a crowbar and a hammer. I didn't know exactly what I would need, but I wanted to be prepared, and I quickly carried all three back out.

She was coming.

She was already walking around the side of the garage. This close, her face not in shadow but illuminated by the full glow of the porchlight, I could see those enormous hairy eyebrows over her still-sleepy eyes, those strange protruding lumps on her skin. She hadn't been smiling before, but she was smiling now with those stained rectangular teeth, a loose casual grin akin to the amiable nonchalance of her walk, and it was all I could do to force myself to drop the crowbar and hammer and grip the ax with both hands.

I'm not a hardass. I've never been in the military, and I'd certainly never killed anyone before. But I felt no qualms as I lifted the ax and swung it at that impossibly deformed head. She—it—saw me but made no effort to stop or run or move out of the way, and I hate to admit it but I felt a sort of grim satisfaction as the blade chopped through cheek and nose and embedded itself in skull. *This is for Ed,* I thought. *This is for Judy.*

I'd been half-afraid that she would keep walking, that nothing would be able to stop her, but she crumpled on the spot, nearly pulling me down with her until, at the last second, the ax blade was freed from her skull with a sickening squeak of bone. There was no blood, no slime, no liquid of any kind that spilled from the gaping wound, and I waited there for a moment but she didn't move.

Now I was in a hard spot. In movies, this was where the hero walks away while, behind his back, the supposedly dead monster gets up and comes back to life. I didn't want to make that mistake, but I didn't have the stomach for chopping her up.

What were my choices, though? I could reach down and see if I could feel a pulse or a breath to see if she was still alive—but maybe she'd never had a pulse, maybe she'd never been alive, and maybe that was when she would suddenly grab my hand and pull me on top of her.

I stood there for a moment, then stepped back and gathered up my courage and prodded her with the blunt edge of the ax blade. No movement, no reaction. Still, I couldn't be sure she wouldn't spring up and attack, and though the fire was gone from my belly and I no longer had any desire for violence, I picked up the ax and chopped off her head. It wasn't just one whack, like you see in the movies. My first swing went halfway through, exposing corded muscle and a segment of white spine. No blood still, but at least the interior of the neck looked the way it was supposed to. I pulled the ax out and up, did it again, and this time it went nearly all the way through. There was only a little bit of flattened skin at the bottom that was connecting the head to the body, but one more chop took care of that, and I used the ax to push the head away.

I picked up the crowbar and the hammer. It was time to put an end to all this.

I hurried next door. On the other side of the professor's house, I saw darkness moving over the roof and walls of Tony and Helen's place. It looked at first like it was being engulfed by some sort of monstrous shadow, but when I got closer I saw that it was a tidal wave of black bugs that were swarming over their home. Whatever it was, I was certain that it was connected to the shrine, and the sight of it spurred me onward, made me run faster. Or as fast as I could while carrying the tools. This time, I didn't care if I bumped into objects on the way, and I dashed through the side yard, not slowing down when I reached the back. I slammed into an unseen tree stump, nearly tripped over a hose and a rake, but I stumbled and stabilized and kept going.

Lights in the professor's house were on, I noticed. I thought of that transparent woman strolling through those filthy rooms, and the image of it chilled me to the bone. For the first time that evening, I saw this as though it was happening to someone else. I was in a fucking horror movie. I'd just been lurching from one thing to another since the Pittman kid (what the *hell* was his name?) first ran up to me on the street, but now I realized how much had happened, the extent of the power I was up against. I pushed the thought away, not wanting to be intimidated by what I was about to face.

I reached the shrine.

It looked even spookier to me than before, but I didn't give myself time to think about it. I dropped the ax, shifted the hammer to my left hand and swung the crowbar with my right. The adobe was already old and crumbling, and my blow chipped off a large piece at the top. There was a shape carved into that rounded section of the shrine, a strange-looking spiral, and the second that it was cut in half by my crowbar, I thought I felt and heard a deep rumble, almost like a sonic boom, but maybe it was just my imagination.

That was it, though.

I guess I'd expected some sort of…defense. I thought the shrine or whatever sentient power lurked within the black space of that deep alcove might make an effort to protect itself. But nothing tried to stop me as I went at it with both hands, crowbar in the right, hammer in the left. I felt like John Henry or something, a superhuman man, and the shrine broke into pieces before my furious onslaught, chipping away bit by bit until only the alcove itself was left standing.

I kicked away the photos and the fingernails and the petition and tried to tear apart the rounded alcove, but that thing was tough. It was not adobe like the rest of the shrine, but it was not metal or wood or cement, either. I couldn't tell what it was made of. All I knew was that my blows were having little or no effect on it, and I was feeling increasingly uneasy standing in front of that black open space.

I dropped the hammer and moved around behind the alcove, stepping over the rotted boards of the collapsed playhouse and balancing on a cobweb-covered log that had rolled off the woodpile some time ago. The alcove was black in back, too, only there were symbols written on it. Symbols and what looked like words in a foreign alphabet. They were almost as dark as the dome-like structure itself, and I probably wouldn't have noticed them if they hadn't reflected the moonlight. I wondered if they were written in blood.

I remembered what had happened when I broke off that symbol at the top of the shrine, and whether that sonic boom was in my imagination or not, I had no other ideas or plans, and I used the crowbar to start chipping away at the squiggly characters. This worked better. The metal crowbar smashed into and smudged a strange triangle-looking symbol, and all of a sudden a crack appeared in the top of the alcove. I hit one of those foreign words, and a piece of its backing flaked off, spiraling to the ground. I smelled shit and rotten eggs, and I thought that *this* was the alcove's defense mechanism. Like a skunk, it was trying to chase me away with foul odors, and that made me work even harder. I started *wailing* on that sucker, and was rewarded with almost immediate results. With each letter or symbol that splintered off or was scraped away, the alcove seemed to weaken and buckle until finally it collapsed in on itself with a noise that sounded more like the scream of a woman than the crack-clunk-thump of shattered stone hitting the ground.

I leaped out of the way, the log rolling beneath my feet, and stumbled through the rotten wood of the playhouse until I was once again in front of the structure. Or what used to be the structure. There was nothing left but what looked like a pile of jagged black rocks. In the rubble, I saw what appeared to be a burnt Barbie on top of a wiggly slice of cheesecake. I don't know if it was alive, but it was moving, twisting around in slow motion like it was doing tai chi, making a sound like a rusty hinge. I couldn't see any eyes, couldn't see any facial features, but I could tell that it was look-ing up at me, and that gave me the eeri-est feeling I'd ever had. I shivered. The doll smiled at me, and in the moonlight I saw one bright white tooth.

I batted that fucker to Kingdom Come. The crowbar hit its midsection, and it flew apart, body cracking in half, legs breaking against black stone rubble, arms shattering into pieces, split head flying off into the dark. The cheesecake beneath it splattered everywhichway, and left in the center, on a small piece of crust, was a nasty black beetle with furiously snapping pincers. I smashed it with the crowbar, then smeared its guts around to make sure it was gone for good.

I looked down at my feet. The photos and fingernails had scattered, but the petition, oddly enough, had been blown back onto the little flat slab of adobe that used to stick out in front of the alcove and was now the only thing left standing. I raised my crowbar high and brought it down on that small slab, grateful to see it shatter.

The shrine was gone.

"Take that," I said.

I was out of breath and breathing like a mother, but I backtracked up the path and walked up the steps into the house, just to make sure it was all over. I wasn't afraid anymore, in fact I half-expected to find the transparent woman dead and dissolved, but she was in that first filthy bedroom and very much alive, and she attacked me the instant I stepped through the doorway. She was wearing the bloody nightgown that had been thrown over the chair, and she jumped me, knocking me to the ground. The light was on, so I could see her clearly, and she wasn't wielding any type of weapon, so I instinctively let go of the crowbar and reached up to grab her wrist.

Big mistake.

She was off me and rolling, surprisingly fast for someone so large. She grabbed the crowbar off the floor and ran with it to the bed, moving expertly around all the books and newspapers and magazines on the stained carpet. She turned around and swung, the crowbar whistling as it cut through the air, and I could see that she was crying. Her tears were invisible on that transparent skin, but the redness of her eyes and the quivering of her lips gave it away.

"Which one are you?" she demanded.

I shook my head.

"Which one *are* you?"

"I'm Gil Marotta," I said.

She backed around the bed until she was in the corner, sobbing, feebly swinging the crowbar, holding it in both hands. I could have rushed her and taken it from her. I could have killed her. But I decided to leave her alone and call the cops when I got home.

I turned to go, and a book hit me in the back of the head. A big book. It knocked me forward, stunned me, and another one followed immediately after, this one hitting at an angle and drawing blood. I whirled around, arms up to protect myself, ready to fend off another book or even a full-frontal assault if I had to, but she wasn't throwing books at me anymore and she wasn't rushing me with the crowbar. Instead, she'd fallen forward onto the bed, the crowbar on the mattress next to her but no longer in her hands. I ran forward, grabbed it, backed away.

She lay there unmoving.

Was she dead? I didn't know. I didn't think so, but I was not about to check.

I kept backing up, moving slowly so I didn't trip over any of the crap she'd left on the floor of that pigsty.

Power had a cost, and while I would never know for sure, I was willing to bet that was what had happened to her, that was why she had become transparent. Whether she provided the shrine with its power and was drained of it herself, or whether she had worshiped at that black empty space and a sacrifice had been demanded of her, the two were connected.

She moaned, lifted her head, looked at me.

I left the room, walked onto the porch, walked down the steps. It was over, it was finished. I'd call the cops from home, I decided, let them take care of her.

I felt exhausted, as though my body had been put through a wringer, but I thought about Lynn and Frank and smiled to myself. At least they were safe, at least they were all right.

I trudged across the circle to my house. And my family.

PLEASE RETURN ITEMS IN OUR
BOOKDROPS
09/28/2020 16:47
Dover Public Library
Library hours: Mon-Tue 9-8:30
Wed - Fri 9-5:00, Saturday 9-5
library.dover.nh.gov

Main Desk: 516-6050
Children's Room: 516-6052
Reference: 516-6082
Checked out to Card Number: 1708

The haunting hour
Barcode:34505001984861 Date Due: 10/19/2020

The circle
Barcode:34505003285739 Date Due: 10/19/2020

The Halloween tree
Barcode:34505003852819 Date Due: 10/05/2020

Overdues
PLEASE RETURN ITEMS IN OUR
BOOKDROPS